GOING TO
SCHOOL
IN 1776

John J. Loeper

GOING TO SCHOOL IN 1776

ILLUSTRATED WITH OLD WOODCUTS

Atheneum 1974 *New York*

Acknowledgments

The author wishes to thank Old Sturbridge Village for permission to quote from *Town Schooling in Early New England*. Also the Historical Society of Pennsylvania for permission to use quotations from issues of the *Pennsylvania Magazine of History and Biography*.

The author also wishes to thank the Historical Society of Pennsylvania, the Bucks County Historical Society, the State Library of New Jersey, the David Library of the American Revolution, and the New England Historic Genealogical Society for the use of their research facilities.

Although based on historical fact, names and incidents are ficticious.

TO JANE

A teacher in spite of herself

Contents

GOING TO
SCHOOL
IN 1776

Introduction

In 1776, a girl wrote this verse on the first page of her copybook:

> *The grass is green,*
> *The rose is red,*
> *Remember me*
> *When I am dead.*
>
> RUTH WIDMER

History is not just facts. History is people. It is made up of girls like Ruth Widmer, who once were but are no more. It is a record of living and a chronicle of lives.

If a generation gap can divide generations, how much

more can a time gap divide people? We are separated from the America of 1776 by two centuries of social, political, and economic growth. The task of history is to bridge that gap and bring real people who were into touch with real people who are.

Our awareness of 1776 is overwhelmed by the political and military drama of the American Revolution, and rightly so. Yet, throughout that year, ordinary people did ordinary things. This book is about one of those ordinary things—going to school and growing up in 1776. It is a remembrance of children, like Ruth Widmer, and the activities that filled their lives.

The World of 1776

If we were to journey back over the highways of history to the year 1776, we would find that most people lived on farms or in small villages. Even cities like Philadelphia, New York and Boston were small. Only two million people lived in America, compared to the over two hundred million here today. Life was much different then. There was no electricity, no indoor plumbing, and no automobiles. Rooms were heated with wood fires and lighted by candles. Travel was mainly by horseback over narrow, dirt roads.

Yet, in 1776, history was being made around the globe. Powerful men and women sat on the thrones of Europe, and in America, a new country was about to appear.

As the year dawned, Catherine the Great was empress of the vast Russian holdings. She spent the winter months in her palace at St. Petersburg, returning to Moscow in the spring. Frederick the Great ruled in Germany and was engaged in building a Prussian empire. The Hapsburg Empire, including Austria, Hungary, and Bohemia, was controlled by the aging Maria Theresa and her son, Joseph II. And in France, Joseph's sister, Marie Antoinette, was at Versailles, the queen of Louis XVI. Her life of gay parties and court balls would end in 1793, when she became a victim of the French Revolution.

It was also a time when men entertained new ideas. The works of the philosophers Locke and Voltaire were widely read and admired. Both men preached democracy and the concept of individual liberty. Locke was especially admired and would be called the Philosopher of the American Revolution. "In the long run," he wrote, "the people can be trusted to judge what is best for them."

It was also a time rich in the arts. The young Mozart was enchanting Europe with his music, and Gilbert Stuart was in London studying art under Benjamin West. Stuart would paint portraits of the Revolutionary heroes. In Scotland, Robert Burns was writing his Highland poetry, and in Boston, the patriot silversmith, Paul Revere, was creating bowls and candlesticks that would rest someday in museums.

And on the island of Corsica, a little boy was celebrating his fifth birthday. Someday he would topple thrones and change the face of Europe. His name, Napoleon Bonaparte.

Many colonists talked of "liberty," "independence" and "revolt." They were growing weary of Britain's rule and their spirit was that of Patrick Henry—"Give me liberty or give me death!" In England, King George and his Parliament responded with more troops and more taxation.

The year 1776, in the last quarter of the eighteenth century, was ripe with promise and change.

As 1776 arrived in the New World, it was snowing in New England and the Southern fields were glazed with frost. As the colonists awoke to the start of a new year, they sensed that it would be a year of decision. For as the snow fell and the winter winds blew, there were rumblings of war and revolution. British troops occupied the city of Boston, and a new American army was drilling under the command of General George Washington. The year before, American blood had been spilled at Concord and Lexington, and American and British troops had clashed at Fort Ticonderoga.

When a pamphlet was published early in 1776, the sentiments of American patriots were stirred. It was Thomas Paine's *Common Sense*. In it, he called Britain an "open enemy" and said, " 'Tis time to part. . . . The authority of Great Britain over this continent . . . must have an end." The response to *Common Sense* was immediate and contagious. Feelings reached the danger point. At the very same time, King George III concluded a contract hiring 30,000 German soldiers. These Hessians were to help him put down "those rebellious Americans." The whole country was aroused by the King's action.

Meanwhile, in Philadelphia's State House, the Second Continental Congress, representing the thirteen colonies, struggled to put the feelings of the colonists in writing. Five members were selected to do the job. There was wise old Benjamin Franklin of Pennsylvania, John Adams of Massachusetts, Robert Livingston of New York, Roger Sherman of Connecticut, and Thomas Jefferson of Virginia. Day by day they wrote and pondered. Finally, by the end of June, they presented their Declaration of Independence to the Congress.

A few days later, John Adams wrote to his wife Abigail, "Yesterday, the greatest question was decided that was ever debated in America. A resolution was passed without one dissenting colony, 'that these United Colonies are and ought to be free and independent states.' It is the will of heaven that these two countries should be sundered forever."

America and England finally separated. The bell atop the State House pealed the news of liberty.

In Philadelphia, the *Evening Post* reported:

> At twelve o'clock today, the Declaration of In-
> dependency of the United States of America was
> read to a large number of the inhabitants of the
> city and was received with applause and heart-
> felt satisfaction. And in the evening, our Late
> King's coat-of-arms was brought from the hall
> in the State House and burned amidst the accla-
> mations of a crowd of spectators.

The decision to separate from England ripped the colonies apart. Bitter feelings were generated, and a large
number of people wanted to remain loyal to their king.
They had little sympathy with their rebellious countrymen. One loyalist lamented, "I am a lover of peace, what
must I do? . . . If I attach myself to the Mother Country, which is 3,000 miles away, I become an enemy to my
own region; if I follow the rest of my countrymen, I become opposed to my King."

But war had come. Already a fleet of British ships,
laden with Hessian soldiers, had sailed into New York
harbor. The King would not give up the colonies without
bloodshed!

During the fall and early winter, American and British
troops met in battle. At each step, the Americans seemed
to lose ground. Washington and his army were in retreat
from New York, while a weak Congress tried to hold the
colonies together. Things looked bleak indeed!

It was not until Christmas night, when Washington and

his ragged army crossed the Delaware River to attack Trenton, that the situation improved. The victory at Trenton echoed up and down the colonies. As 1776 drew to a close, the patriots began to take heart. Perhaps there was hope ahead, after all. Perhaps the dream of a free and independent America would come true.

That was 1776. Yet, as battles raged and men struggled with political ideas, daily life went on. The struggle was still young and the hardships of war were yet to touch the entire population. Still ahead was the bitter winter at Valley Forge and the occupation of Philadelphia. Far ahead was the victory at Yorktown. For many colonists, at least for the present, life had not been altered by the ravages of war. Despite it all, houses were built, fields were plowed, and children went to school.

Being a Child in 1776

It is dark when Johnathan's mother calls him and he is
forced to leave the warmth of his bed. He throws back
the covers and is at once exposed to the chill of his bed-
room. Then, walking to the window and drawing aside

the homespun curtains, he peers out into the darkness beyond. Only a trace of yellow-pink haze over the horizon tells that it is morning. Below, he can hear the rattle of milk pails and the crunch of his father's footsteps as he walks over the hard snow toward the barn. Downstairs, pleasant noises come from the kitchen as his mother prepares breakfast. There will be johnnycake, mush, and fresh milk. It is the start of another day.

Johnathan lives in the colony of New Hampshire. This colony was settled only three years after the Pilgrims landed at Plymouth. His parents moved here from the neighboring colony of Massachusetts in 1768. They settled on a farm near Portsmouth in the Salmon River valley.

Once, Johnathan visited Portsmouth with his father. A thriving seaport town, Portsmouth is an exciting place to see. There are many shops and beautiful homes. Portsmouth also has shipyards that build big sailing vessels. Johnathan enjoys watching the men fit boards tightly together to make the hulls and decks, while others stitch

heavy canvas for the billowing sails. But the family seldom leaves the farm now and Portsmouth seems far away. With trouble brewing in the colonies, his father says it is best to stay at home.

When Johnathan finishes dressing, he hurries down to the kitchen. It is warm there, and he is very hungry. The wood in the fireplace crackles and the delicious aroma of cooking fills the small kitchen. The johnnycake sits on a clean ash board before the fire, while a kettle of mush bubbles and hisses.

His sister, Elizabeth, dresses the little ones in a corner of the room and has to scold them for not holding still. Johnathan has three younger sisters.

When his father comes in from the barn, the family gathers around a plank table. After a blessing, there follow the dull clatter of pewter spoons in pewter bowls and talk of the day's assignments. Elizabeth will have to work

at the spinning wheel while Johnathan carves new rake handles with his barlow knife. When these chores are finished, both of them will walk to Mistress Robbins' house for their daily lessons. As the little ones are too young for school, they will remain at home.

In 1775, many New England towns closed their schools for the duration of the war. With the local school closed, Johnathan and his sister must attend a "dame school" for the time being. These are schools run at home by some older women in the community. Mistress Robbins has ten pupils, ranging in age from seven to fourteen years. Johnathan does not like Mistress Robbins, as she has only rough slabs for seats and, when you misbehave, she pins you to her apron. Under this arrangement, you can hardly move, and her apron smells of grease. The younger pupils are taught how to read and sound out alphabet letters, while the older ones memorize passages from the Old Testament. She also teaches everyone, including the boys, how to sew and knit.

Johnathan and Elizabeth will remain at Mistress Robbins' until late afternoon. Then, they will walk home through the woods and across the open fields. It will be a long walk and both of them will arrive home tired and hungry.

After a hearty supper, the family will gather around the fireplace to talk and exchange stories before going to bed.

❋ ❋ ❋

Johnathan's cousin, Abraham, lives in the city of Philadelphia in the Pennsylvania colony.

Life in a city is much different. There are many shops and theaters and taverns and many of the streets are paved with cobblestones. There is even a building in Philadelphia where you can pay admission to see tigers, lions, and polar bears. In Philadelphia, people carry a new invention when it rains. It is called an umbrella. The citizens of this city take great pride in their sophisticated ways. John Adams calls it "the happy, the peaceful, the elegant, the hospitable, and polite city of Philadelphia."

Philadelphia is also a hub of political activity. The Continental Congress is in session there, and there are visiting delegates from all over the colonies.

Many of these patronize Abraham's father, who owns a livery stable. They may have read his advertisement in the *Pennsylvania Packet*:

> *George Fell, No. 124*
> At his livery stable, in Pine, near Fifth Street, begs to inform the public that he has for hire a number of genteel carriages—such as coaches, chairs, and traveling chariots, with sober, careful drivers. Also good saddle horses are always ready at the call of those who may please to employ them, either to go on journeys or use about the city. He begs that his low fees and his close attention to customers will recommend him to the notice of the public.

Each morning Abraham walks to the stable to help his father. His job is to brush the horses with a currycomb and rub grease into the leather harnesses until they glisten.

Following this, he walks through the narrow streets to school. He attends Mr. Buller's school in Strawberry Lane. Mr. Buller teaches boys "writing, arithmetick, accounting, navigation, algebra, and Latine." School starts at eight in the morning and goes until noon. It resumes again at two in the afternoon and closes at five. There is even school on Saturday.

Mr. Buller is a stern master. He believes that busy boys cannot make mischief. He insists that all the lessons be neatly copied in a copybook. This way, they can be studied at home. His students are expected to be "as quiet as a mouse and as industrious as a beaver."

The master also believes in rules and regulations. Abraham was given a printed list of "Rules to be observed by the Scholars" on his first day at Mr. Buller's. Among the many rules are:

> That no Boy shall absent himself from the School without producing a note from one of his parents.

> That in coming to School and in returning home everyone shall behave with Decency and Sobriety, and give no offence.

> That in their conversation, they shall be careful never to utter any rude or uncivil expression, nor call their Schoolmates by a nickname.

> That in their hours of leisure, they shall avoid ranting Games and Diversions and Quarreling with each other.

Once, Abraham quarreled with a classmate and found that Mr. Buller meant what he said. The other boy's father is a loyalist, and Abraham's father is for independence. When the boy called General Washington a "damned rebel," Abraham punched him. Mr. Buller found out about the quarrel and locked both of them in a dark closet for an entire afternoon. Despite his admiration for the General, Mr. Buller enforced his rules. "Rules are not made to be broken," he insists.

❊   ❊   ❊

Every morning, young George Hawkins arises at dawn and goes downstairs to light a fire in the fireplace. He has to have the front room warm for Mr. Marker. Then he and Nellie, Marker's black servant, eat breakfast together in the kitchen. It is always the same—a mug of strong, hot tea and a piece of freshly baked bread. He enjoys eating breakfast with Nellie. She has a wide smile and calls him her "sweet Georgie." Sometimes, as a special treat, she bakes sugar muffins for him. Nellie is his good friend.

After breakfast, George hurries along Duke of Gloucester Street toward Mr. Marker's cabinet shop. He passes the King's Arms Tavern and waves to Billie, who works in the apothecary shop. The day starts early in colonial Williamsburg.

Williamsburg is the capital of colonial Virginia and was named in honor of King William III. From its very beginning, it took its place as one of the most important centers of culture and commerce in the colonies. William and Mary College is there, as is the Governor's Palace and the House of Burgesses. It was here that young Patrick Henry delivered his famous "liberty or death" speech.

The people of Virginia colony love their land and fiercely support the cause of independence. Many Virginians are among the early American patriots. The names of Washington, Jefferson, Monroe, and Lee are well known in Williamsburg. Once, George saw Mr. Jefferson come out of Chowning's Tavern with a group of young gentlemen.

When George reaches his destination, he lays out the tools for the day's work. This is a part of his responsibility. Today, they will finish the armchair for Mr. Wythe and start work on a new table for the Raleigh Tavern.

Although George is only twelve years old, he is Mr.

Marker's apprentice. After years of training, he will become a cabinetmaker himself and perhaps open his own shop.

Under the apprentice system, boys are trained for some skillful occupation. An agreement is signed that has both the boy's consent and that of his parents. The term of service runs from four to seven years, and during this time the apprentice lives in the master's house. Besides teaching him a craft, the master also agrees to instruct him in the three Rs ("reading, 'riting and reckoning") and provide him with adequate food and clothing. In return, the apprentice promises to be obedient, dutiful and loyal.

George's legal agreement, called an indenture, reads:

> This Indenture witnesses that George Hawkins,
> Son of Phineas Hawkins, hath put himself, by

and with the advice and consent of his Father, and of his own Free Will and Accord, as apprentice to Samuel Marker.

During the term of this agreement, the said Apprentice shall do no harm or damage to his said Master and shall serve him faithfully. He shall not waste his Master's goods nor lend them to anyone.

He shall neither buy nor sell without his Master's approval. He shall not absent himself from his Master's house without the Master's permission. He shall not play cards, dice, or other improper games. He shall not visit Ale-houses, Taverns, or Playhouses. He shall not marry.

And the said Master shall teach the said Apprentice the trade or mystery of cabinetmaking. He shall provide for him sufficient meat, drink, apparel, lodging and washing. He shall also teach him reading and accounting at leisure and shall provide him with proper books and paper.

In 1776, there are thousands of boys apprenticed to craftsmen. In the absence of vocational schools, this system allows young people to learn a trade or some skillful occupation. Often, girls are apprenticed to older women to learn the "arts of housewifery." Many girls marry when they reach sixteen.

Three signers of the Declaration of Independence had been apprentices. Benjamin Franklin had apprenticed in the printing trade, Roger Sherman had apprenticed as a shoemaker, and George Walton of Georgia had apprenticed as a carpenter.

Someday, when young George Hawkins is a master craftsman himself, he, too, will have a young apprentice. Then he will teach him the "mysteries" of the trade. He will show him how to turn a lathe, how to join wood, and how to plane a board. But that is years away. Right now, there is work to be done before Master Marker arrives at the shop.

❋   ❋   ❋

Amid the bustle and noise of the Baltimore waterfront, nine-year-old Elias Penrose watches the great ship *Duchess of Somerset* prepare to set sail for England. At high tide, she will glide out of the harbor to cross the wide Atlantic. Aboard will be Elias and his family. They plan to leave America to live in Herefordshire, an English county on the Welsh border. Here, in the Wye River valley, where his father was born, Elias and his brother will live and go to school.

Elias's father is leaving America with his family because he is not in sympathy with the Declaration of Independence. The thought of rebellion and revolution angers him, and he wants nothing to do with the separatist cause. He is loyal to his king and to his birthright as an English citizen. After the Declaration of Independence was signed, he made arrangements to leave the country. Although he has been in America for twenty years, this voluntary exile is his form of protest.

There are thousands upon thousands of loyalists like

him. Many are prosperous citizens and community leaders. Some will seek refuge in England and Canada, while others will remain in America and join forces with the British troops against the revolutionaries. Not all the colonists favor independence.

As Elias watches his father supervise the longshoremen loading the family's possessions on board ship, he is touched by a certain sadness. He must leave his friends behind, and he will miss them.

Yet, the ocean voyage should prove exciting. He has never sailed the seas, and this will be a new experience.

In a few short hours, standing on the deck of the *Duchess of Somerset,* Elias will watch the shores of America slip from view. And, as his father has explained to him, they will leave behind "a land where reason has given way to bloodshed and treachery."

How Children Dress in 1776

ABOUT SAMUEL PEMBERTON'S WIG.

ABOUT SALLY RAWSON'S NEW DRESS.

HOW WILLIAM FREEMAN DRESSES FOR HIS PORTRAIT.

WHAT MRS. WINSLOW ORDERS FROM LONDON.

AN ITEM FROM THE *Essex Gazette*.

Although he is only ten years old, Thomas Pemberton wears a wig. One day, a barber shaved his head, and the local wigmaker fitted him with a wig. It was so heavy and uncomfortable that it made Thomas complain, "My head itches and aches like anything!" Yet, boys of wealthy families have to be in style!

Of course, Thomas does not wear his wig all the time.

Around the house or at play, he covers his shaved head with a pretty embroidered cap. In winter, he exchanges this for one made of fur.

In 1776, it is fashionable for upper-class gentlemen to wear wigs. Called "perukes," the wigs are made of natural hair and are powdered white. They are then braided and ribboned. Sometimes, a long pigtail is fashioned in back, then looped and tucked in a small silken bag. The fashion of wearing wigs originated in France but soon spread to the New World. Wigs are quite common among the upper classes, and the practice of wearing them will not die out until after the Revolution.

As Thomas's father is a successful merchant, he can afford to dress his son well. In his ruffled shirt, velvet knee breeches, and powdered wig, Thomas is a proper little "gentleman." In 1776, the manner of your dress indicates your social position.

Unlike Thomas the sons of plainer folk wear their hair short-cropped. Their shirts are made of homespun and their breeches of buckskin. More practical clothing is needed for doing daily chores.

❊　❊　❊

October 19, 1776, is a very special day for Rebecca Rawson. It is her eleventh birthday and she is quite excited.

She had asked for a new dress and her mother had located several lengths of blue satin at Mr. Holt's shop on Canal Street. Fancy cloth is hard to find because it has to be imported and the war has interrupted regular shipping.

A few months earlier, an English cousin had sent a doll

dressed in the latest London fashion. This is one of the ways that colonial ladies keep abreast of new designs from abroad. When Rebecca first saw the doll's dress, she hoped for one just like it. Her mother promised to copy it and give it to Rebecca as a present.

She cut the fabric to Rebecca's measurements, and the sewing began. Everything had to be done by hand, and even Rebecca helped with some stitching. Finally the dress was ready—in time for her birthday, just as promised. When she tried it on, Rebecca was delighted. Like the doll, she now has a rich, full-skirted overdress of deep blue. It brushes the ground when she walks, revealing a petticoat underneath, of a lighter shade. Her long sleeves

have wrist-ruffles and the neckline of the dress is low and round. It, too, has a ruffle. With her new gown, Rebecca plans to wear a big, feathered hat and high-heeled shoes. She will also wear a pair of gold earrings, a gift from her grandmother.

In 1776, older children are dressed as miniature replicas of adults. It is not until after 1800 that more practical clothing is designed especially for children.

* * *

Another birthday gift in 1776 is a portrait of little William Freeman. His father commissioned an artist to paint a likeness of William as a present for his mother.

The artist is an itinerant painter. He earns his living by traveling from place to place, painting landscapes, doing portraits, and decorating inn signs. He stopped by in William's village and started his work. Each morning, William poses for his portrait. It is very hard to stand still, especially when your nose itches or the kitten wants to play.

The portrait is completed in less than two weeks. The artist works quickly, and although it is no great work of art, it is at least a good likeness. William's mother will have a picture of her son to hang on the sitting-room wall.

As William is only five years old, he still wears baby clothing. For his portrait, his mother dressed him in a long linen frock with many petticoats. Over this he wore a waistcoat with silver buttons and lace cuffs. Very young children like William wear long dresses, often edged with lace and heavily embroidered. Both boys and girls dress very much alike until they are six. Then, they go directly into adult clothing.

   The finished portrait shows William in his fine dress
against a background of dark green. In his right hand, he
holds a small basket of fruit. Although his head and hands
seem too large for his body, William's mother is pleased,
and her husband gives the artist an extra shilling for doing such a fine job.

In another part of the American colonies, a candle flame
flickers as the movement of Mrs. Winslow's quill pen stirs
the air. She is writing a letter to a friend in Britain, asking her to purchase some clothing for her daughter, Lucy.
The letter will leave the next day on the sloop *Good
Hope,* bound for London. Mrs. Winslow will deliver the
letter personally to the ship's captain. With luck, the
ordered items might arrive at the Winslow residence in
Baltimore by early next year. Sailing vessels do not travel
quickly and the political situation might delay shipment
even more than usual.

Many colonial ladies, like Mrs. Winslow, prefer to purchase some things from London. Not only is it more fashionable, but, often, the quality is much better.

Here are some of the things that Mrs. Winslow ordered
for Lucy:

> *six pairs of fine cotton stockings*
> *one pair of white kid gloves*
> *one pair of silver shoe buckles*
> *six handsome egret plumes*
> *four yards of crimson ribbon*
> *one satin capuchin (a hooded cloak)*
> *two cambrick (fine, white linen) petticoats*
> *one pair of very thin shoes of morocco leather*
> *six carved buttons*

Yet, just as today, the America of 1776 is populated by
different people with different ways. Not all of them dress
as well as Lucy, in fine London fashion. There are many

who wear simple clothing. One report confirming this says, "Children wear leather aprons reaching from their chins to their ankles. The aprons are striped and shining with bean porridge, which in winter makes the principal food of the children. Many of the little girls take snuff; it is the fashion. The boys wear leather aprons and breeches. The girls wear loose gowns and skirts and woolen stockings. They wear blankets over their heads or their mother's old cloaks. In summer they wear gowns and skirts and cape bonnets, with bare feet. You might as soon look for a white bear as to see shoes on children in summertime."

❋   ❋   ❋

Item from the *Essex Gazette*, January 18, 1776.

January 7, 1776

This morning, the sixth daughter of Captain Bancroft of Dunstable, Massachusetts, was baptized by the name of Martha Dandridge, the maiden name of his Excellency General Washington's lady. The child was dressed in buff and blue, with a sprig of evergreen on its head, emblematic of his Excellency's glory and provincial affection.

The Schools of 1776

ABOUT COLONIAL EDUCATION.

HOW SILAS ATKINS HATES HARROW HALL.

A SCHOOL IS BUILT IN NEW JERSEY.

ABOUT THREE LITTLE GIRLS ON A PLANTATION
    IN NORTH CAROLINA.

DR. FRANKLIN RECALLS HIS SCHOOL DAYS.

In 1647, a Massachusetts law required every town of at least fifty families to hire an elementary teacher and build a school. Every town of one hundred families or more was to have a Latin grammar school. This idea soon spread to other New England colonies.

The New England schools were public schools, open to

all children. They were operated by the town fathers, but families who could afford it were asked to pay tuition. As New England was largely Puritan, religious teachings were an important part of what the children learned. Nor did the citizens object to the use of some public tax money for the cost of these schools. Religion and education seemed to go hand in hand.

In other colonies, like New York and Pennsylvania, there were several different church groups. Each church wanted its own doctrines taught and would object to the use of any public money to promulgate another religion. Under such circumstances, it was impossible to set up a public school system. As a result, each church operated its own schools. If a child did not attend a church school, the only other school available was an independent one. There were many of these independent schools, operated by ministers or other interested citizens. Benjamin Franklin, for example, started his own academy in the 1750s.

Education supported by public money did not gain favor in all the colonies until long after the Revolution. In some states it was almost a century before schools were free to every child. Willing citizens had to "subscribe" to a school. Parents who "subscribed" paid tuition for their children and were responsible for the upkeep of both the school and the schoolmaster. If there was no school building, then they had to build one. Once built, the prosperity of the school depended on the prosperity of the subscribers.

In the Southern colonies, wealthy planters hired their own teachers and operated their own schools. With few exceptions, poor children in the South did not go to school.

In the elementary schools, children learned reading, writing, arithmetic, and religion. After three or four years, their formal education was finished. Then the boys might begin to learn a trade, either with their fathers or apprenticed to some other man. A few boys, whose parents wanted them to become lawyers or ministers, went on to a Latin grammar school. There, they learned to read, write, and speak Latin. A knowledge of Latin and Latin literature was the mark of an educated man.

Education, beyond learning to read and write, was mostly for the upper classes. It was less for women and seldom for blacks.

❊ ❊ ❊

The morning dew lies heavy on the grass and birds are beginning to wake and twitter. Day is breaking, a day in mid-April, 1776.

Young Silas Atkins sits up in his narrow, wooden bed and looks out into the uncertain, gray light of early morning. The other boys in the small dormitory room are still asleep, but not for long. Soon, Mr. Watts will ring his bell to signal the start of another day at Harrow Hall.

Silas hates Harrow Hall! If he had his way, he would be spending his day as a farm hand or a stable boy in General Washington's army. But, his father sent him to Harrow Hall last year, and here he must remain. From here, he will probably go on to Harvard or Yale.

Harrow Hall is a private boarding academy kept by a minister, the Reverend Isaac Watts. It is really Mr. Watts' own home, but he calls it an academy. His method

of imparting knowledge is by "God and rod." The school days are filled with long sermons, many prayers, and frequent floggings.

In the letter Mr. Watts wrote to Mr. Atkins before Silas enrolled, the characteristics cultivated at Harrow Hall were listed. "My scholars will be Amiable, Benevolent, Conscientious, Forgiving, Grateful, Humble, Industrious, Mannerly, Obedient, Punctual, Quiet, Responsible, Studious, and Truthful." In an opposite column were listed the "evils" that would not be tolerated. "They shall not be Heedless, Selfish, Disobedient, Revengeful, Unthankful, Arrogant, Slothful, Disrespectful, Thoughtless, or Lazy."

To achieve these goals, the boys sit eight hours a day on hard benches, studying grammar, reading the Bible,

and memorizing hymns. To gain their complete coopera-
tion, Mr. Watts gives them a "brisk slap on the ear or
face, for something or nothing—next thing to be seen is
a strap in full play, over some head and shoulders." He
struts about the room shouting, "Be busy! Be busy!",
accompanying his order by striking the desks with a huge
hickory stick.

The school day at Harrow Hall starts at sunrise with
morning prayers, and closes at sunset with evening prayers. After this, the boys go directly to bed. The daily
meals are mostly brown bread, pork, porridge, and beans.
Occasionally, beer is served. Beer is a common drink for
all ages.

School is held six days a week, Monday through Saturday. Sunday, however, is no day of rest. There are prayer
meetings in the morning, and a long sermon in the afternoon, delivered by Mr. Watts himself. In a roaring voice,
he reminds the boys of their evil ways and the necessity
of constant discipline. He also reminds them of their good
fortune to be at Harrow Hall under his special guidance.
Silas does not agree!

In 1776, many parents want their children surrounded
by religion, and taught religion in the strictest manner
possible. Mr. Watts, and others like him, serve that purpose. The fear of the Lord, they believe, is the beginning
of wisdom.

✳　✳　✳

In 1776, Silas Thompson and a group of other interested
citizens of Monmouth County in the New Jersey colony
decide to build a school. Despite the war, they need a

schoolhouse, and they have already found a suitable teacher. They obviously heed the advice of a local almanac that warns, "The wise man will do three things to prepare for the winter: secure his floor from frost, fasten his shingles, and find a good school for his children."

The first step is to find a suitable location. At a meeting held in Silas Thompson's farmhouse, everyone present agrees that the schoolhouse should be centrally located. Everyone also agrees that it must be built on worthless land. "Why waste good farmland on a schoolhouse?" one farmer asks. After much debate, a location is found. The school will be built close to the main road on a rocky stretch of land. This is not too unusual.

One observer of the times notes, "Of the schools I visited, nineteen are located directly in the highway. Thirteen are bounded by two roads. None has any shade trees or any of those adornments which are resorted to to make our homes pleasant and healthy." No one could accuse schools of having any "frills" in 1776!

The school will be constructed of logs with a plank floor. The roof will be made of roughly hewn shingles, and the interior walls will be plastered with a mixture of mud, straw, and animal hair. These walls will be whitewashed later on. Four windows with glass panes are planned along with a plank door and a stone threshold.

The schoolhouse interior will be one large room with a fireplace to provide warmth. Since many schoolhouses are unheated, this will be a luxury. Each subscriber has promised to provide firewood during the winter months as part of his children's tuition. One farmer is making benches for the scholars and a desk and stool for the master. This will be the only furniture. A local glassblower has promised to provide inkpots.

When the schoolhouse is completed, it will house fifteen local children. The youngest child will be seven and the oldest, sixteen.

On a warm, spring day while the delegates in Philadelphia debate independence, three little girls sit in the music room of their plantation home in North Carolina. One is playing the harpsichord, a stringed instrument that looks somewhat like a piano. Another is playing the harp, while the third plays a flute. All three have taken music lessons ever since they were small. They practice daily and are accomplished musicians! Today, they are playing a piece from George Bickham's *Musical Entertainer,* a popular music book published in London about 1740. Their selection is called, "The Compassionate Maid." As the one plays the music on the harpsichord, she sings the words:

> *See Phyllis in yonder bower,*
> *With every beauteous flower,*
> *And twining green arrayed.*
> *Sweet jonquils, daffodillies,*
> *Carnations, roses, lillies.*
> *Invite us to the shade.*
> *Invite us to the shade.*

When they finish with their music, they will walk to the central hall of the house and ascend the wide staircase to an upstairs room, that serves as a schoolroom.

Their home is resplendent with polished furniture, fine carpets, draperies, and costly ornaments imported from Europe. They live in comfort and leisure.

There are many great Southern families who live like lords, keeping packs of choice hunting dogs and stables of blooded horses. They travel about in a coach-and-six, and their spacious mansions are built of imported brick. Within are grand staircases, marble mantles and carved mahogany paneling. The sideboards glisten with silver and crystal and the tables are loaded with luxuries from the old world. Black servants throng about, ready to perform any service.

The girls' father is a wealthy planter. He owns an im-

mense tract of land and has many black slaves to plant
and harvest his crops. These large, slave-worked farms are
known as plantations. The father is also a member of the
Provincial Congress of North Carolina. Only large land-
owners may be members of the Congress. Right now they
are meeting in Halifax and intend to instruct their delegation to the Continental Congress in Philadelphia to
vote in favor of independence.

Once in the schoolroom, the girls are joined by children
from neighboring plantations. Several planters in the area
joined together and hired a teacher for their children. The

girls are taught reading, writing, and fine stitching. The
boys are taught reading, writing, and bookkeeping. Their
lessons last only an hour.

As there are few teachers in the Southern colonies, these
children are most fortunate to have a classroom. Many
Southern children have only "field schools" to attend.
These are informal and infrequent lessons taught in the
open fields by some interested adult.

One of the most respected citizens of 1776 is Dr. Benjamin Franklin. He is a friendly man with a ready wit, and an easy smile. A Philadelphia businessman, he is one of America's leading statesmen as well as an accomplished writer, inventor and scientist.

He served as the first Postmaster General of the American colonies, having been appointed to that post by the King in 1753. Now, however, he is dedicated to the American cause and serves as a member of the Pennsylvania delegation to the Continental Congress.

One evening, in April of 1776, Dr. Franklin and Mr. Robert Morris, another member of the Pennsylvania delegation, go to Mr. Thorne's school in Vidall's Alley. Mr. Thorne has offered his school to the delegates as a meeting place. While there, prompted by his surroundings, Dr. Franklin recalls his own school days:

I was sent at the age of eight years to a grammar school. My father destined me for the church, and already regarded me as the chaplain of the family. From my infancy I had learned to read, for I do not remember to have ever been without this acquirement. My father was convinced that I would one day certainly become a man of letters. My uncle Benjamin approved also and promised to give me all his volumes of sermons, written in a shorthand of his own invention, if I would take the pains to learn it.

I remained, however, scarcely a year at the grammar school, although in this short time, I had risen from the middle to the head of my class. But, my father, burdened with a large family, took me from the grammar school and sent me to a school for writing and arithmetic, kept by Mr. George Brownwell, who was a skillful master. Under him, I soon acquired an excellent hand; but I failed in arithmetic and therein made no sort of progress.

Mr. Morris laughs, and remarks that, despite his failure in arithmetic, he has little trouble adding up his many successes. Dr. Franklin responds by quoting from his *Poor Richard's Almanac,* "Remember, Mr. Morris, God helps them that help themselves."

The Teachers of 1776

SILAS CROCKER LOOKS FOR WORK.

MISTRESS ROBBINS WRITES IN HER JOURNAL.

MR. HART ADVERTISES FOR A "RUNAWAY SCHOOL-
TEACHER."

It is noon when Silas Crocker reaches the wooden tollgate
on the dusty, rutted highway leading westward.

He had set out early this morning on foot, carrying the
greater part of his wardrobe on his back, with the remainder tied up in a cloth sack. Winter is coming, and it is time
to find a school.

Mr. Crocker is an itinerant schoolteacher, going from
village to village in search of employment. During the
summer months he earns a living plowing, mowing, and

carting manure. In the winter, he teaches school. Having the reputation as the greatest "arithmeticker" in the county, he is a respected schoolmaster. Most of the schoolrooms in the area are familiar with this tall, gaunt master.

Because the toll keeper is known to Mr. Crocker, he shares some news with him from Boston. He has heard that General Howe ordered "linen and woolen goods, articles much wanted by the rebels and aiding and assisting them in their rebellion," be seized and "kept out of rebel hands." Mr. Crocker, being sympathetic to the American cause, replies that the rebels might have his woolen coat if it would help put down the British. He adds that he has considered joining the militia and might do so if he can't find a school. Many schoolteachers have joined General Washington's army. One, a John Downey of Philadelphia, is already a captain.

After paying a penny toll for the use of the road, the teacher walks on, waving good-bye to his friend in the tollhouse. The late September sky is bright with sunshine but a chill breeze warns of winter. Soon the ground will harden and cold winds will strip the trees. He must find a school.

With the harvesting almost over, the children are ready for their winter lessons. Perhaps the next village will need him.

❋ ❋ ❋

From Mistress Robbins' Journal.

> My name is Elizabeth Robbins, and I am in my seventeenth year. I have been engaged to teach at Litchfield. A committee of the subscribers examined me and asked that I read passages from

the Old Testament. They seemed pleased when I did not stumble over the big words. They asked for samples of my penmanship, which I showed, to their satisfaction. When convinced that I had sufficient knowledge to keep school, I was hired for a period of five months, at four dollars a month. I am to board about in the homes of the scholars, and pay each family seven cents a week for my washing.

When I arrived at Litchfield to commence my duties, I came to stay with Mr. and Mrs. Benning. The family consists of the man, his good wife, daughter Polly, Caesar the dog, and a number of cats. My room has a broken window, which I stuff at night with my coat, in order to keep warm. The food is plentiful, but poorly cooked. Often I feel as though I have eaten a section of stone wall! Each evening, after supper, Mr. Benning leads us in prayers and hymn singing.

I find a wretched schoolhouse, in the road, as it were, with a tiny fireplace. At first, it was easy, as the older scholars stayed away. When the school is full, however, it is very difficult to teach. The older boys make many threats against me. They are generally lawless, and in the habit of using profane language. I have to resort to using severe corporal punishment to maintain order.

I start my day at sunrise. My duties include sweeping and cleaning the schoolroom and setting the fire. In the morning, I teach the beginners while the older ones copy in their books. After recess, there is a general spell for the remainder of the morning. The afternoon is for reading and catechism. I am not obliged to teach arithmetic.

I will not be unhappy to leave Litchfield and the following winter I hope to take a school near Newburyport.

❊　❊　❊

On December 21, 1776, an advertisement appears in the *American Daily Advertiser*.

WANTED

Ran-Away from the subscriber, an indentured schoolteacher named SILAS LEWIS, about 24 years of age. It is likely he will change his name. He had on when he ran away a cloth jacket and dark trousers. He is five feet and four inches in heighth and of heavy build. All vessels and others are forbid harboring or carrying off said man.

John Hart
No. 2 South Second Street, Philadelphia

In the eighteenth century, indentured labor is a term used for immigrants who come to the American colonies under contract.

An indenture is the name for a legal document. It can be a deed or a contract. Two copies of the terms are made on the same sheet of parchment. The parchment is then divided with a knife in an irregular cut. In case of dispute, the two pieces can be fitted together again. If they fit exactly, it proves that the documents are original. This is the way records are kept and authenticated in 1776.

It is not uncommon for wealthy gentlemen and businessmen to pay passage to the New World for certain men and women from abroad. These, in turn, sign a contract promising to work for a term of years. This repays the cost of their passage. For many men and women, this is the only way they can afford to emigrate. They are called indentured servants and are bound to their masters under the law.

Silas Lewis was brought to Philadelphia by Mr. Hart in 1773 for a term of seven years. As he can read and write well, having been educated in England, Mr. Hart hired him out as a teacher in his children's school. Many indentured servants, if educated, are assigned to teaching positions.

But Silas was not happy. He wanted his freedom. He knows that he has an obligation to Mr. Hart, but he yearned to be his own master. Someday, he hopes to repay Mr. Hart in another way.

Many indentured servants share the same longing as Silas. The newspapers have many advertisements asking for the return of runaways.

Perhaps Silas will be found and brought back to Mr. Hart. There are many who feel that he has already joined the Continental Army under an assumed name. Mr. Hart says that if this is so, he will gladly give Washington another soldier, since he is a champion of the American cause.

The School Books of 1776

ABOUT SCHOOL BOOKS.

LESSONS FROM ISAAC GREENWOOD'S READING BOOK.

PROBLEMS FROM DAVID BUTLER'S CIPHERING BOOK.

ABOUT THE *New England Primer*.

School books were not plentiful in 1776. Many of them were shared by several children and used over and over again by different classes. Paper was in short supply and printing was expensive.

There were scholars who never had a printed textbook of their own and relied entirely on dictation from the teacher's single copy.

Among the available textbooks were spellers, grammars,

readers, and "arithmetickers." Geography and history texts were less common.

The school books of 1776 reflected the codes and customs of their time. Many of the lessons ended in a moral or stressed certain religious and social principles. From the Quakers of Pennsylvania to the Puritans of New England, elders expected children to value virtue and goodness.

Upon opening a school book, one could often find an inscription on the flyleaf. This identified the book's owner and might carry a message in verse. Often, it was a warning not to steal the book or a plea to return it, if lost.

As school books were scarce, this was a necessary precaution.

✳   ✳   ✳

Isaac Greenwood is my name,
Steal not this book for fear of shame.
And if this book should chance to roam,
Just box its ears and send it home.

HIS BOOK, 1776

Lesson Two

1. It is winter. We will sit by the fire and tell stories.
2. Take care, Martha, you stand too near the fire. You will burn your toes.
3. We will have some pudding and Silas may have some beer.
4. It is dark now; light the candle.
5. The sun is gone to bed; the chickens are gone

to bed. Little boys and girls must go to bed.

6. Poor little Silas is sleepy. He must be carried upstairs. Pull off his shoes.

7. Pull off his frock and petticoat. Put on his nightcap. Lay his head on the pillow and cover him up.

8. Good night, little Silas.

Lesson Seventeenth—
The Rooster, the Cat, and the Young Mouse.

A young mouse, that had seen very little of the world, came running one day to his mother, in great haste.

"Oh, mother," said he, "I am frightened almost to death! I have seen the strangest creature that ever was. He has a fierce, angry look, and struts about on two legs. A strange piece of flesh grows on his head, and another under his throat, both as red as blood. He flapped his arms against his sides, as if he intended to rise into the

C   Cock.   c

air, and stretching his head, he roared at me. I trembled and ran as fast as I could.

"If I had not been frightened by this terrible monster, I would have formed a friendship with the prettiest creature you ever saw. She had soft fur, thicker than ours, beautifully streaked with gray and black. She had a modest look and a humble manner. She was so courteous that I could have fallen in love with her. She had a long tail which she waved about prettily, and I do believe she was going to speak to me when the monster frightened us away."

"Ah, dear child," said the mother mouse, "you have escaped being devoured, but not by the monster who frightened you. He was only a rooster and would have done you no harm. The sweet creature, of whom you seem so fond, was no other than a cat, who hates us and lives by eating mice. Learn from this, my dear child, never rely on outward appearances. Things are often not what they seem to be."

❊ ❊ ❊

Whoever steals this book away,
Will find on that great judgement day,
That the Lord will come and say,
"Where is that book you stole away?"
Then you will say, "I do not know."
And He will say, "Go down below!"

DAVID BUTLER'S BOOK, 1776

Ciphering Problems

1. John made 3 marks on one leaf of his copy-book and 6 on another. How many marks did John make? ($3 + 6 = 9$ marks)

2. The mistress punished him for soiling his book. She gave him 3 blows on one ear and 3 blows on the other ear. How many blows did John receive? ($3 + 3 = 6$ blows)

3. There were 7 farmers who drank rum and whiskey and became miserable. The other farmers drank water and were healthy and happy. If there were 10 farmers altogether, how many drank water? ($10 - 7 = 3$)

4. John the Baptist was beheaded in 32 A.D. and the Book of Revelations was written in 87 A.D. How long after John the Baptist was be-headed was the Book written? (55 years later $87 - 32 = 55$ years)

5. If a farmer's wife wanted to dye her wool red and needed one quart of pokeberries boiled in one quart of water for every 20 yards of thread, how many pokeberries must she gather to dye 100 yards of thread? ($100 \div 20 = 5$ quarts)

* * *

The most widely read and influential textbook in 1776 was the *New England Primer*. It was first compiled by Benjamin Harris, a Boston printer, and was published around 1680. First used in the New England colonies, the Primer was revised and reprinted many times. Eventually it spread throughout the colonies.

The Primer was small, a book of about eighty pages, and was called "The Little Bible" by some schoolmasters. It was illustrated with blurred woodcuts, usually depicting some biblical scene. In 1776, its front page showed a picture of King George III, but, following the Revolution, this was changed to one of George Washington.

The Primer began with the alphabet and a table of easy syllables. *Ab, eb, ib, ob* and so forth. It moved on to a list of harder words, going to words of six syllables. Then, there were morning and evening prayers. One of these, especially loved by children, was, "Now I lay me down to sleep."

After the prayers was a set of little rhymes, one for each letter of the alphabet. This was the heart of the Primer and the way that children learned their letters. Examples are:

A — In *Adam's* Fall We Sinned all.

B — Thy Life to Mend This *Book* Attend.

C — The *Cat* doth play And after flay.

D — A *Dog* will bite A Thief at night.

E — An *Eagles* flight Is out of fight.

F — The Idle *Fool* Is whipt at School.

A In Adam's fall,
   We sinned all.

G As runs the glass,
   Our life doth pass.

P Peter denied
   His Lord, and cried.

Y Young Samuel dear,
   The Lord did fear.

Z Zaccheus he,
   Did climb a tree,
   His Lord to see.

The book continued with biblical quotations and pious stories about martyrs and Old Testament heroes. It concluded with the Lord's Prayer and the Apostle's Creed.

The *New England Primer* was used by generations of schoolchildren. It lasted well into the nineteenth century. More than three million copies were printed before it passed out of use.

The Lessons of 1776

Timothy Mather's father claims that "The Holy Book and figgers are all I want my boy to know!" Evidently, he believes that these are two essential academic skills. So Timothy had better learn to read and figure.

Timothy attends a local school where the lessons are taught by the "blab" method. The teacher gives the lesson, and the children "blab" or shout it back in unison.

"One, two, three," says the teacher.

"One, two, three," blab the children.

"Four, five, six," continues the teacher.

"Four, five, six," blab the children.

"Now, all together," the teacher instructs.

"One, two, three, four, five, six," blab the children.

To help the little ones learn more easily, the teacher puts the lesson in rhyme.

> *"One, two, how do you do?*
> *Three, four, my feet are sore.*
> *Five, six, gather sticks.*
> *Seven, eight, lay them straight.*
> *Nine, ten, start again."*

Timothy enjoys the rhyme and blabs it over and over again. Within a short time, he will learn the lesson. As a wise saying promises, "Repetition is the mother of learning."

In 1776, the "blab" is a common teaching method. A nicer term for it is "class recitation."

⁕ ⁕ ⁕

Nine-year-old Mary Howe takes her quill pen and dips it carefully into a small inkpot. She has practiced her penmanship on her slate and is now about to copy an example of it in her copybook.

In 1776 many children have copybooks. As writing paper is scarce, a copybook is a precious possession and

Emulation Seldom fails

Remember thy creator in the days of thy youth

only the best examples of schoolwork are entered on its blank pages. Fine examples of penmanship are prized.

In a beautiful, practiced hand, Mary copies her sample. It is a virtuous saying that the teacher dictated. On the page, with many lovely scrolls and flourishes, Mary writes, "Who tries again, will surely win."

As she writes, she recalls the stories her father told her last night of General Washington and his brave men. The news from New York is not good. The General and his army are in retreat through New Jersey. But Mary is certain that the General practices this virtue. He will try again, and he will surely win.

As if to encourage him from afar, Mary writes it once again on the page. Underneath, she adds a thought of her own. "God bless good General Washington."

❊   ❊   ❊

Edward Jackson lives in Rhode Island. In school, he has learned about New England. Let's listen to his answers as his teacher questions him.

"Edward, what colonies comprise New England?"

"New England is composed of Maine, Vermont, New Hampshire, Massachusetts, Connecticut, and Rhode Island."

"Who are the inhabitants of New England?"

"The inhabitants of New England can be divided into three classes: savages, civilized, and enlightened. Indians are savages. The settlers are civilized, and the inhabitants of Boston are enlightened."

"What is the chief occupation of the New England people?"

"Their chief occupation is farming."

"Why is farming a noble occupation?"

"Because it is the most necessary, the most healthy, the most innocent, and the most agreeable occupation."

"Why is farming the most innocent occupation?"

"Because farmers have fewer temptations to be wicked than other men. They work dawn to dusk and spend little time in idleness."

"What is the temper of the New England people?"

"They are bold and enterprising. The women are educated to housewifery, spending their time in sewing and cooking. The men-folk are industrious and sober, being good farmers and fishermen."

The teacher is very pleased with Edward. He has learned his lessons well.

Fourteen-year-old John Cheever attends Harvard College. He came here from the Boston Latin School. A knowledge of Latin is necessary in 1776 for entrance to Harvard, for Latin is considered the language of scholars.

It is not unusual for young teen-age boys to be enrolled at a college or university, because there is no intermediate schooling available. John sits at a small table in his room and writes a letter to his father.

Dearest Father,
You were pleased to know that I could decline all my Latin nouns, conjugate all the verbs, both regular and irregular, and possess an entire vocabulary of Latin words.

Now you will be pleased to learn that I have followed Caesar on his wars and Aeneas on his adventures. I can read the poet Horace with ease and have begun to read the history of Livy. I enjoy it greatly.

"Hoc illud est praecipue in cognitione rerum salubre ac frugiferum, omnis te exempli documenta in illustri posita monumento intueri."

Your loving son,
John

In the last paragraph of his letter, John quotes the Roman historian, Livy. "This above all makes history useful and desirable: it unfolds before our eyes the glorious record of the past."

The Discipline of 1776

RICHARD HALL IS PUNISHED FOR FIGHTING.

WILLIAM RODMAN WEARS A DUNCE CAP.

MASTER LOVELL'S DESCRIPTION OF A "BAD BOY."

"The spirit of the times has caught up with the school-boys," writes Master Fisher in his journal. "They carry on clandestine battles with each other, with one group being the British and the other being the Colonials."

Richard Hall, always eager for a fight, is the leader of the colonial side in this contagious game of war. He is opposed by the older boys, who are playing the British.

At the first encounter, held in the west field behind the schoolhouse, the "British" force the Colonials into retreat.

As the defeated side run toward the schoolhouse, Richard Hall turns and throws a heavy mudball at Henry Harmon, the "British" general. It splatters all over his shirt, and when Master Fisher sees it later, he demands an explanation.

Upon questioning, Richard Hall is identified as the culprit. Master Fisher goes no further. He needs only one guilty party to make an example to the others. And it is not the first time Richard has fought with his classmates.

"I forbid quarreling in my school," he reprimands the boys. "And you, Richard Hall, are guilty of misconduct. You will be humbled before your fellows."

In the center of the schoolroom, there is a post, going from floor to ceiling. Primarily intended for support, the post has been put to another purpose by Master Fisher. He uses it as a whipping post. Richard is ordered to stand by it and grasp it firmly with both hands. With Richard thus positioned, Master Fisher lashes his back with a birch branch. With swift and sure strokes, Richard is "humbled."

The Master says that "God made the birch for many good uses, and none better than for the beating of stubborn boys, who quarrel and will not follow rules."

✳ ✳ ✳

Poor William Rodman! He has not learned his ciphering. The question he cannot answer:

> If ten angels, blowing on ten golden trumpets, are needed for each of the five continents to wake the dead on Judgement Day, how many angels must the Lord dispatch?

William cannot compute the answer of ten times five, or fifty angels. He turns a blank expression toward the teacher and squirms slightly on the bench. He knows the consequence of not answering! It is not the first time. William has trouble with arithmetic.

Within the next few minutes, William finds himself seated on the dunce stool, wearing a conical dunce cap. Around his neck is a placard marked with the degrading name of "Baby-Good-for-Nothing." He will be forced to sit here for the rest of the day and endure the teasing of both teacher and pupils.

In 1776, dunce stools are a cruel, yet common punishment. Their purpose is to embarrass a child into learning. If he cannot succeed, he is made to look ridiculous before

THE BETTMANN ARCHIVE

the rest of his classmates. Sometimes, a special dunce stool is used. Called a unipod, it is a stool with a single leg and requires a good sense of balance. If the victim falls from it, he is ridiculed even more or may be beaten by the teacher.

"The children are pleased with corrections," writes one schoolmaster, "and thankful to pay for their errors."

Right now, William Rodman would not agree.

The embarrassment of being the dunce is degrading and the name "Baby-Good-for-Nothing" will ring in his ears for a long time. And when his parents hear of it, he will be punished again at home.

❋　❋　❋

Master Lovell, a schoolmaster of East Haddam, Connecticut, writes this description of a "bad boy" and offers his remedy.

A Bad Boy is undutiful to his father and mother, disobedient and stubborn to his master, and ill-natured to all his playmates. He hates his books and takes no pleasure in improving himself in any way. He is sleepy and slothful in the morning, too idle to clean himself, and too wicked to say his prayers.

He is always in mischief, and when he has done a wrong, will tell twenty lies to clear himself. He hates to have anyone give him good advice, and when they are out of sight, will laugh at them. He swears and wrangles and quarrels with his companions, and is always in some dispute or other.

He will steal whatever comes his way; and if he is not caught, thinks it no crime, nor considers that God sees what he does. He is frequently out of humour, and sullen and obstinate, so that he will neither do what he is asked, nor answer any question put to him.

In short, he neglects everything that he should learn, and minds nothing but play and mischief. He grows up a confirmed blockhead, incapable of any thing but wickedness and folly, despised by all men of sense and virtue, and generally dies a beggar.

To avoid coming to this end, and to make a bad boy into a good one, he should be thrashed daily for some reason or other, and locked securely in a closet. There he can meditate upon his sins and thus avoid his fate.

Being a Girl in 1776

TRAINING FOR PROPER YOUNG LADIES.
ABOUT MARY MARSHALL'S NEEDLEWORK.
ABOUT EMILY ROBINSON'S SAMPLER.
POLLY WHARTON'S LETTER.

In 1776, both boys and girls were taught to read and write in the common schools. It was considered proper that girls write a "fair and legible hand." Beyond this, their education was usually confined to the "female arts"—music, dancing, religion and needlework. The latter was most important. Knitting and sewing were vital in a homespun society, where clothing was manufactured at home.

Not only to sew, but to turn a fine stitch, was the ambition of most proper young ladies. Many of their completed projects were stored away in hope chests to take with them when they married. This was their contribution to a new home.

* * *

Every afternoon, following her lessons, just as the winter sun filters through the parlor windows, young Mary Marshall sits by the fire to do her knitting. It is her favorite time of day, a quiet, pleasurable period when both mind and fingers find rest in the steady rhythm of knitting.

Right now, Mary is finishing a pair of long stockings, using silk in an openwork design. The silk was brought to her from across the seas by her uncle, who is a sea captain. The stockings will be a wedding gift for her older sister, who plans to marry Quentin Singer, a cavalryman of General Washington's guard.

Using delicate bone needles, Mary's deft fingers transform the thread into a delicate lace.

Mary can also do tambourwork, a method of darning decorative designs on cloth. She has made several tambour pillowcases for her mother. Still another talent is her Turkeywork, and an example of this graces the upholstered chair in her bedchamber. Turkeywork is a needlework imitation of designs from Turkish carpets and is made by knotting colored yarn on heavy cloth.

Mary finds both amusement and satisfaction in her needlework. It helps to pass the long winter days, and it bestows a sense of womanly accomplishment. Her mother claims that Mary's long slender hands have "true sewing fingers."

To complete her talents, Mary hopes to learn feather-work. Yesterday she read an advertisement in the *Gazette:*

> Martha Creedon is now in the city to teach the following works: all sorts of needlework, feather-work, crewelwork and painting on glass. If any young Gentlewoman is inclined to learn the above-mentioned, she will be carefully and diligently instructed by the same Mrs. Creedon.

As she read it, Mary hoped that her father might allow her to study with Mrs. Creedon. Featherwork is the art of sewing feathers on cloth to form flowers, birds, and other decorations.

Mary has a box of feathers that she has collected over the years. There are bright bluejay feathers and some exotic ones of scarlet and yellow. Then she can decorate a bonnet for her mother and a sash for herself.

* * *

A sampler is an exercise in needlework that shows a girl's ability to execute various stitches.

The word comes from the Old French word, "essam-plaire," and the Middle-English word, "samplere." It is a practical demonstration of skill, and the young girls of 1776 take great pride in their needlework samplers. To them, a sampler is akin to a final examination in stitchery.

Most samplers contain the alphabet, the numerals one to ten, and a verse, either biblical or contrived. The sampler is then signed and dated.

Some samplers are decorated with geometric designs or

with representations of flowers, fruits, animals, trees and people. Some ambitious examples might illustrate Adam and Eve in the Garden of Paradise or the myriad animals aboard Noah's Ark.

A sampler is done on either bolting cloth or tammy cloth. The former is a silk-textured material that has been dipped in gum water to add body. Tammy cloth is a heavy woolen-linen mixture. A few samplers are done on canvas.

On a sampler, the alphabet and numerals are done in cross-stitch. This is the basic embroidery stitch. However, fancy stitches are used for embellishment. Among these are the chain stitch, the tent stitch, the eyelet stitch, and the French knot. It is claimed that there are more than twenty stitches a girl can execute in working her sampler.

Emily Robinson's sampler is a rectangle of tammy cloth, measuring six inches by fourteen inches. At the top, she has placed the date, 1776, in a cross-stitch of red thread. Below this is the alphabet in a cross-stitch of bright blue. Near the bottom of the sampler, embroidered in a violet thread, is a verse of Emily's own composition. It is surrounded by a narrow border of tiny, colored flowers. The verse reads:

Emily Robinson is my name
America is my nation
Remember me when this you see
For Christ is my salvation.

When I am dead and in my grave
This needlework will tell
That I tried to do my very best
And learned my lessons well.

Wrought by Emily Robinson

When Emily marries, her framed sampler will occupy a place of honor on the sitting-room wall. It will serve as her certificate of merit in needlework, and her own daughters will want to emulate their mother's skill.

* * *

On Christmas Day, 1776, while Washington and his army wait on the icy slopes of the Delaware, preparing their march on Trenton, young Polly Wharton, sitting in a nearby house, writes a letter to her cousin, Mary.

Dearest Mary,

This Christmas day is cold and bleak. It snowed yesterday and the fields are deep in drifts. There are many soldiers about in the woods and fields near the river, and some officers stopped by yesterday to ask for food. Father gave them a basket of eggs. One of the young officers was very handsome despite his ragged appearance and he smiled at me.

I have stayed indoors and passed my time in sewing and reading, with Tabby, the cat, by my side. After my embroidery, I read first from the Bible and then from father's copy of Mr. Foxe's

Book of Martyrs. I also read from Mr. Jane-way's *A Token For Children.*

He teaches us that laziness is the worst form of sin; that good children must rise early and be useful before going to school, and do their chores at evening. He tells us to love the Lord and serve our elders.

I confess that I often feel an unwillingness to do good duties, and I often avoid doing my chores. Yesterday, I concealed myself behind a door, while mother sought me out to help in the kitchen. I know it was wicked of me, but, at times, I confess I find wickedness more attracttive than virtue. Though I am well in body, I question whether I grow in grace.

Do write to me of your activities. I love to receive letters better than I love to write them. Father says that letters are the messengers of the mind and bring friends closer together.

As ever,

Your dearest Polly

Having Fun After School in 1776

TELLING ABOUT FOOTBALL AND OTHER PAS-
TIMES.

HOW THE BOYS AT LATIN GRAMMAR SCHOOL
PUBLISH A NEWSPAPER.

HOW SARAH MOLTON AND HER FRIENDS
KNOW TEN SINGING GAMES.

ABOUT FUN ON THE FRONTIER.

The children of 1776, like children of all ages, found enjoyment in games and simple pastimes.

Little girls blew soap bubbles and baked mud pies, while
their older sisters played hop-scotch. The boys expended
their energy in playing games of tag.

Football was a popular sport in 1776, but of a much different variety from football today. It was played in city streets and on broad country fields with an inflated leather bag. This was kicked about from one boy to another in a rather haphazard fashion. It was a rough game, and many parents complained that it was "nothing but fury and violence!"

Playing marbles and flying kites were warm-weather diversions for both boys and girls.

During the winter months, of course, sledding took over, with children of all ages coasting down hills and slopes. Their sleds were made of wood with wooden runners, and were guided by sharp sticks.

Ice skating was also a cold-weather pastime, especially among the Dutch in New York. The frozen ponds and rivers were often crowded with youngsters wearing either wooden or metal skates.

There were also toys and dolls. Some were crudely made, perhaps whittled out of a piece of pine or manufactured at home. There were cornhusk dolls, whistles, and tops.

Other more sophisticated toys were brought by sailors and sea captains from faraway ports. Before the war, colonial newspapers frequently advertised, "Imported Toys for Children," and Boston had a flourishing toy shop.

✳   ✳   ✳

The colony of Pennsylvania, founded by William Penn in 1681, is mainly a Quaker settlement. Members of the Society of Friends, called Quakers, came to the New World to practice their religion in freedom and escape persecution.

The Quakers established many schools and placed a high value on good education. One of these schools, and one highly esteemed, is the Latin Grammar School of Philadelphia.

In December of 1776, a group of boys from the Latin Grammar School decided to assemble a school newspaper. Sam Wharton is selected editor. The boys call their creation the *Public School Intelligencer,* and its publication is strictly an after-school activity. The masters offer little support in fostering any such frivolous activity during the school day.

The newspapers are hand-written on fourfold sheets of foolscap, a crude paper. They are usually stained by inkblots. The boys take turns writing out each page and some are neater than others!

One of the *Intelligencer*'s features is "Ricker's Riddles," composed by Philip Ricker. Unfortunately, the reader unable to solve the riddles must consult the author for the answers, since they do not appear anywhere in the paper. One of his latest, which has everyone mystified, is:

"Why is thy hat, friend, like a butcher shop?" No one but Philip knows the answer, and he refuses to tell!

Another very popular section is the gossip page. Here, Sam Wharton reports on happenings around the Latin Grammar School. In the first edition, he observes:

> "Last week, the boys were led to Meeting by Master Thomas. He was unaware that, behind his back, the line of young Quakers carried wooden guns and little flags, pretending to be a line of British soldiers.
>
> On Monday last, two boys of no name bored a hole in the classroom ceiling through which they extended a long cord and hook. On this, they hoisted aloft the curled, grey wig of Master Robert, leaving it suspended from the ceiling and Master Robert much angered.
>
> Which boys disassembled a farmer's wagon on Friday last, and reassembled it on the top of the chimney, to the astonishment of its owner and the amusement of the populace?"

The coin of exchange used by the boys in school is paper, a scarce but necessary commodity. The cost of a subscription to the *Intelligencer* is one sheet of writing paper a week, and an advertisement costs one quarter sheet.

As the boys at the school are likely to lose their books, the newspaper is a handy means of announcing such losses. In one edition, William Helper advertises for the return of his *Coles' Dictionary,* offering a reward of one sheet of paper, while Thomas White offers only a quarter sheet for the return of "one new Greek Grammar."

The paper also advertises other opportunities. Offered for sale in the first edition is "one pack of historical cards" and "one good inkpot."

There is even a sports section, telling that "The boys of this school are entirely taken up with Chuckers, which diversion is continually pursued in the School Yard." Chuckers is a game similar to quoits, where a stone or a penny is thrown, or chucked, into a hole or a container from a set distance.

❊   ❊   ❊

In the late spring of 1776, the days are warm and sunny. It is weather that demands outdoor play, on fields thick with clover and buttercups. The afternoons are long and drift reluctantly into twilight.

On such an afternoon, Sarah Molton and her friends gather on the Shrewsbury Green, to decide which singing game they will play. They know ten of them and each one is as amusing as the next.

"If only the Continental Congress had such easy decisions!" Sarah's mother remarks on watching them.

Amid chatter and laughter, the debate goes on. Some want to play "Here we go round the mulberry bush" or

"Ring around a rosy."

Others suggest "Quaker, Quaker, how art thee?" and "Here I brew, here I bake, here I make my Wedding Cake."

Sarah argues for, "Here come three Lords out of Spain," or "Uncle John is very sick."

Still other suggestions are, "When I was a shoemaker," and "Go round and round the valley."

Finally, a decision is reached. They will play "A farmer went a-trotting." Joining hands to form a circle, they dance round and round singing:

"A farmer went a-trotting,
Upon an old grey mare,
Bumpety, bumpety, bump!
With his daughter there behind him,
So rosey, fat and fair,
Lumpety, lumpety, lump!"

PLATO's SONG.

DING dong Bell,
The Cat is in the Well.
Who put her in ?
Little *Johnny Green.*
What a naughty Boy was that,
To drown Poor Puffy Cat,
Who never did any Harm,
And kill'd the Mice in his Father's
Barn.

Maxim. *He that injures one threat-
ens an Hundred.*

LITTLE

LITTLE *Tom Tucker*
Sings for his Supper ;
What fhall he eat ?
White Bread and Butter :
How will he cut it,
Without e're a Knife ?
How will he be married,
Without e'er a Wife ?

To be married without a wife is a terrible
Thing, and to be married with a bad Wife is
fomething worfe ; however, a good Wife that
fings well is the beft mufical Inftrument in the
World. *Puffendorf.*
SE

SE faw, *Margery Daw,*
Jacky fhall have a new Mafter ;
Jacky mo ft have but a Penny a Day,
Becaufe he can work no fafter.

It is a mean and fcandalous Practice in Au-
thors to put Notes to Things that deferve no
Notice.

Grotius.

GREAT

GREAT A, little a,
Bouncing B ;
The Cat's in the Cupboard,
And fhe can't fee.

Yes fhe can fee that you are naughty, and
don't mind your Book.

SE

Many of these rhymes came down to the children of
1776 from earlier times. Some were brought to America by
early settlers out of the streets of London and Edinburgh.
Others were passed along in early editions of nursery
books, such as *Mother Goose,* printed by John Newberry
of London, about 1760.

Jonah Wells lives in a small cabin clearing on the Allegheny frontier. Here, on the dark edge of the wilderness, life is hard. Young boys must learn to swing an ax, plow a straight furrow, and handle a rifle, while the girls make soap, pound corn, and learn how to bake in outdoor ovens.

On the frontier, children have little time for play. They must find enjoyment in making their own world and in providing for the needs of tomorrow.

When Jonah finishes his lessons at the small "blab" school a mile or so from his home, he must take on his share of providing for the family's needs. One day, it may be to gather the nuts of hickory and butternut trees, while on another it may be to hunt in the leaf-bare woods for wild turkey, deer, or bear. It may be to angle for pike and catfish in cold mountain streams. His chores are half work, half play.

An important part of Jonah's frontier training might be

considered fun by a city boy. Here, it is a necessary accomplishment. He must learn to imitate the calls of wild birds and animals. His mimicry of a pheasant's call may decoy the bird during a hunt. And, by imitating the bleat of a fawn, he may lure a doe to her death. Furthermore, to recognize such mock calls might warn him of unfriendly Indians who use these signals for attack.

Finally, at the close of day, the family may huddle around the hearth to hear the father tell tales of Indian perils or recount the legends of the mysterious West beyond the thirteen colonies.

There is little time for games on the frontier. Fun must be found in the constant struggle for survival.

Our Historical Journey Ends

As we leave the schools and children of 1776 and return to the present day, we sweep past nearly two centuries of American history. Much has happened since that time.

Not only has the nation changed since its beginning, but so has the manner in which we live. Our nation is not the America of 1776, nor is our society the society of 1776. Our homes, our schools, and our way of life have changed.

The schools and the children of 1776 are gone and exist only in the records of history. They can live again only in our imagination. Yet, they are part of this nation's past, and because of this, they are a part of what the nation is today. Though the classrooms and children of 1776 are gone forever, their memory is part of our heritage.

Bibliography

Adams, John and Abigail, *Familiar Letters during the Revolution,* edited by Charles Adams, New York, 1876.

Beattie, James, *James Beattie's Day Book, 1773–1798,* University Press, Aberdeen, 1868.

Collin, Nicholas, *Journal of Nicholas Collin,* New Jersey Society of Pennsylvania, Philadelphia, 1936.

Earle, Alice Morse, *Child Life in Colonial Days,* Macmillan, New York, 1927.

Fennelly, Catherine, *Town Schooling in Early New England,* Old Sturbridge Village, Sturbridge, Massachusetts.

Franklin, Benjamin, *The Works of Benjamin Franklin,* B. C. Buzby, Philadelphia, 1813.

Greene, Evarts B., *The Revolutionary Generation 1763– 1790,* edited by Arthur Schlesinger and Dixon Ryan Fox, Macmillan, New York, 1943.

John Tileston's School, Antiquarian Book Store, Boston, 1887.

Marshall, Christopher, *Diary of Christopher Marshall, 1774–1781,* Albany, 1877.

Morison, Samuel Eliot, *Intellectual Life of Colonial New England,* New York University Press, New York, 1956.

Pratt, Richard, *Commonplace Book of Richard Pratt,* Nicols Press, Massachusetts, 1900.

"Quaker School Life in Philadelphia before 1800," in *Pennsylvania Magazine of History and Biography,* Volume LXXXIX, October, 1965.

Schlesinger, Arthur M., *The Birth of a Nation,* Alfred A. Knopf, New York, 1969.

Shipton, Clifford K., *New England Life in the 18th Century,* The Belknap Press of Harvard University, Massachusetts, 1963.

"Teaching in the Friends Latin School in the 18th Century," in *Pennsylvania Magazine of History and Biography,* Volume XCI, October, 1967.

Wistar, Sally, *Sally Wistar's Journal,* Philadelphia, 1902.